Officer Jack

LOST LADY

By **JAMES BURD BREWSTER**

Illustrated by **MARY BARROWS**

J2B PUBLISHING

Acknowledgement:

This Officer Jack episode is based on a real response performed by Charles County, MD, sheriff's deputies Sergeant C. Black and Officer B. Morrison. The deputies responded to a call from a woman who reported her 81-year-old mother as missing after her mother did not return from her daily walk. The deputies searched the nearby heavily wooded area. When they found the mother, she asked if the deputies were out taking a walk also. When they quietly replied, "Yes," she seemed relieved and told them she had lost her way. "No problem," said Officer Morrison who gently took her hand. He and Sgt. Black walked her back to her house, making small talk and enjoying each other's company along the way. When asked what the key to a long, healthy life was, the woman replied, "Eat good and stay active."

Dedication:

This book is dedicated to police officers everywhere (Federal, State, County, and City) who daily place themselves in harm's way in order to save lives, protect property, and preserve public safety.

Officer Jack and Officer Kate were in Car 14, patrolling the area north of town. It was spring.

"Jack, Stop!" exclaimed Officer Kate, "Look at the cherry trees. They are beautiful!"

Officer Jack checked his mirrors and stopped Car 14. He looked at the trees and smiled.

"Yes Ma'am. Spring around here is very pretty, but Grace School's cherry trees are the prettiest."

Kate nodded. "What's even more beautiful is today's weather. It's just perfect for a walk."

Officer Jack's response was lost in the squawk of Car 14's two-way radio. "Car 14. Come in Car 14. Over."

Officer Kate picked up the microphone. "This is Car 14. Over."

"Respond to the woman at 24 Terrace Avenue," said Dispatch. "She reported her mother missing. Over."

"Responding now!" Officer Kate answered. "Over!"

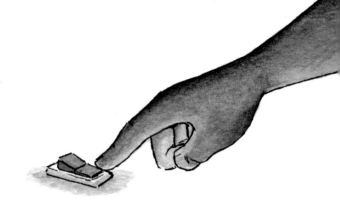

Officer Jack flipped on the lights (Voo, Voo, Voo)

and stepped on the gas (Vrooom, Vrooom).

Drivers in front of Car 14 saw the flashing lights.

They moved to the shoulder of the road to let Car 14 go by.

"Here it is," said Officer Jack as he turned right and drove up a long winding driveway.

A woman waved as they got out of Car 14. "Over here," she called.

Officer Kate spoke first. "Yes, Ma'am. Did you report a missing person?"

The woman said, "Yes, Officer. I'm Sheila Martin. We own this house. It's my mother. She hasn't returned from her walk. I'm worried."

"Please tell us what happened," said Officer Kate.

"My mother lives with us. Every day she exercises by walking down the driveway and back," explained Mrs. Martin. "However, sometimes she forgets things, so we put a fence around the driveway to keep her from wandering into the woods."

"The fence is a good idea," said Officer Jack. "And your driveway is beautiful. She must enjoy the walks."

"She does," said Mrs. Martin. "But she didn't come back today. Something must have happened to her."

"We will do our best to find her, Ma'am," said Officer Kate. "What does your mother look like and when did you last see her?"

Mrs. Martin responded, "She's 81 years old and walks with a cane. She was wearing dark slacks and a light blue floral top. Her name is Betty Andersen. She left about an hour ago. I'm worried she may have fallen."

Officer Jack said, "Please try not to worry, Ma'am. It's a beautiful day, so your mother won't be cold. If she is enjoying the blossoms, she probably won't even be scared."

Officer Jack turned to Officer Kate. "Well, Kate," he said, "You were right. It is a perfect day for a walk. Let's get started."

Officer Kate gave Mrs. Martin a quick hug. "We'll find her," she said. "Our best bet is to start at the end of the driveway. That's where your mother forgot to turn around."

At the end of the driveway, Officer Jack and Officer Kate looked for footprints or bent grass that might show which way Mrs. Andersen had gone.

"Got something," said Officer Kate. "See where the grass is bent and some petals have been stepped on?"

"Sure can," said Officer Jack. "Looks like a faint trail. Let's see where it leads."

The trail headed into the woods and led them around a hill, across a small stream, and to the edge of a field.

An elderly woman wearing dark slacks and a blue floral top stood under the trees at the far end of the field. She hooked a branch with her cane and pulled it towards her. She smelled the blossoms and smiled.

"Beautiful day," Officer Kate said. "How are the blossoms?"

"It's a wonderful day," exclaimed the woman. "And the blossoms are heavenly. Are you out walking, too?"

"We sure are," replied Officer Jack. "May we join you?"

"I'd love it," said the woman. "By the way, my name is Betty Andersen."

"Good to meet you, Mrs. Andersen," said Officer Jack as he introduced Officer Kate.

Mrs. Andersen leaned close to Officer Jack. In a low voice she said, "Maybe you can help me. I usually walk next to a fence and I seem to have lost it. Have you seen it?"

Officer Jack also spoke softly, "We did pass a fence back over there. Shall we see if it's yours?"

Mrs. Andersen straightened up and smiled. "Sounds like a plan," she said.

"Ma'am, the ground here is a bit rough. Would it help you to hold my hand?" asked Officer Jack.

Mrs. Andersen smiled again. "What a splendid idea," she said as she took his hand.

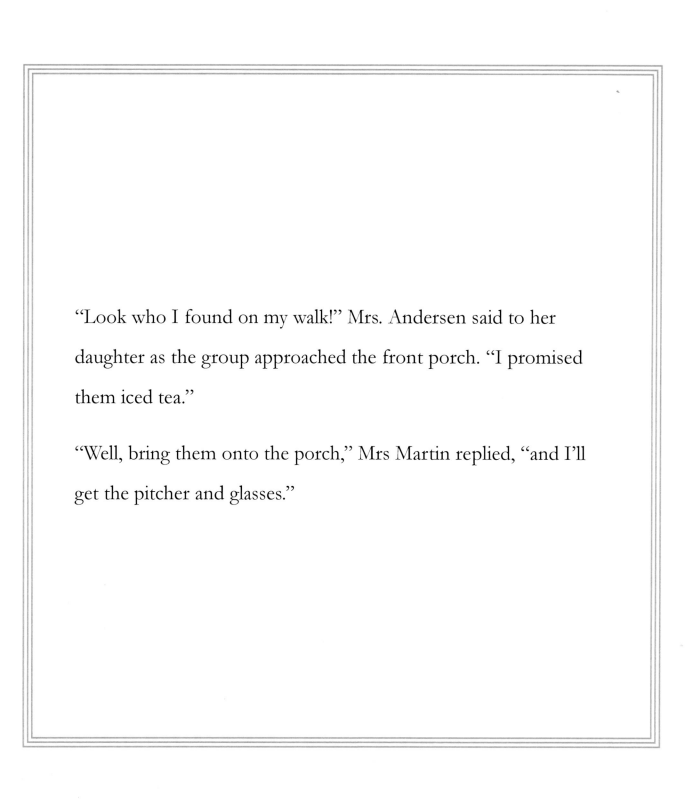

"Look who I found on my walk!" Mrs. Andersen said to her daughter as the group approached the front porch. "I promised them iced tea."

"Well, bring them onto the porch," Mrs Martin replied, "and I'll get the pitcher and glasses."

When their glasses were filled, Officer Jack toasted Mrs. Andersen and asked, "What do you feel is the key to a long healthy life?"

Mrs. Andersen smiled and said, "Eat good and stay active."

Mrs. Martin turned to the officers and said, "Thank you for finding my mother. You are so kind."

Officer Kate thanked God that she had been able to find the trail quickly.

Officer Jack thanked God that Mrs. Andersen had taken his hand.

Officer Jack stood up straight. He gave Mrs. Martin a quick salute and said,

"Glad to do it!"

Meet the Author

James (Jim) Burd Brewster is the author of the Uncle Rocky, Fireman series which are now joined with this book by the Officer Jack series. He was raised in Albany, NY, learned to sail on Lake Champlain, navigated a Polar Icebreaker in the US Coast Guard, and married Katie Spivey from Wilmington, NC. His writing career started when he and Katie took a creative writing class as "Empty-Nesters." Professor Wayne Karlin's class gave him the desire to write down the Uncle Rocky, Fireman stories, Christina Allen's advice gave him the confidence to publish them, and Yvonne Medley's Life Journey's Writers Club gave him the technical knowledge to do it. He can be contacted through: www.gladtodoit.net

Meet the Illustrator

Mary Barrows is a freelance illustrator from the small town of Walkersville, MD. Since she was old enough to hold a pencil, she has been drawing pictures of her favorite stories, and she hasn't stopped yet. She is the second oldest of six kids with a passion for children's books and fantasy stories. When she isn't illustrating, Mary loves to read, play basketball, and mess around on her guitar.